A Note to Parents and Caregivers:

Read-it! Readers are for children who are just starting on the amazing road to reading. These beautiful books support both the acquisition of reading skills and the love of books.

 The PURPLE LEVEL presents basic topics and objects using high frequency words and simple language patterns.

 The RED LEVEL presents familiar topics using common words and repeating sentence patterns.

 The BLUE LEVEL presents new ideas using a larger vocabulary and varied sentence structure.

 The YELLOW LEVEL presents more challenging ideas, a broad vocabulary, and wide variety in sentence structure.

 The GREEN LEVEL presents more complex ideas, an extended vocabulary range, and expanded language structures.

 The ORANGE LEVEL presents a wide range of ideas and concepts using challenging vocabulary and complex language structures.

When sharing a book with your child, read in short stretches, pausing often to talk about the pictures. Have your child turn the pages and point to the pictures and familiar words. And be sure to reread favorite stories or parts of stories.

There is no right or wrong way to share books with children. Find time to read with your child, and pass on the legacy of literacy.

Adria F. Klein, Ph.D.
Professor Emeritus
California State University
San Bernardino, California

Editors: Jacqueline A. Wolfe and Nick Healy
Designer: Tracy Kaehler
Page Production: Lori Bye
Creative Director: Keith Griffin
Editorial Director: Carol Jones
The illustrations in this book were created with acrylics.

Picture Window Books
5115 Excelsior Boulevard
Suite 232
Minneapolis, MN 55416
877-845-8392
www.picturewindowbooks.com

Printed in the United States of America.

Library of Congress Cataloging-in-Publication Data
Blackaby, Susan.
Jake skates / by Susan Blackaby ; illustrated by Troy Olin.
p. cm. — (Read-it! readers)
Summary: Jake loves to skate so much that he skates nearly everywhere he goes.
ISBN-13: 978-1-4048-2412-6 (hardcover)
ISBN-10: 1-4048-2412-X (hardcover)
[1. Roller skating—Fiction. 2. Asian Americans—Fiction.] I. Olin, Troy, ill. II. Title.
III. Series.
PZ7.B5318Jak 2006
[E]—dc22   2006003410

Jake Skates

by Susan Blackaby
illustrated by Troy Olin

Special thanks to our advisers for their expertise:

Adria F. Klein, Ph.D.
Professor Emeritus, California State University
San Bernardino, California

Susan Kesselring, M.A.
Literacy Educator
Rosemount–Apple Valley–Eagan (Minnesota) School District

PiCTURE WiNDOW BOOKS
Minneapolis, Minnesota

Jake loves to skate.

He has black skates with
bright orange laces.

Jake skates everywhere.

Jake skates down Main Street and around the corner.

He stops to get a drink.

Jake skates through the park and along the river.

He stops to feed the ducks.

Jake skates to the playground at his school.

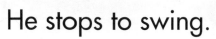

He stops to swing.

13

Jake skates home and up
the driveway.

14

He climbs the steps to go inside.

"Jake, take off those skates,"
says Mom.

"No skates in the house,"
says Dad.

There are some places where Jake cannot skate.

Jake cannot skate at the table. He has to eat.

Jake cannot skate in the bath. He has to get clean.

Jake cannot skate when he goes
to bed.

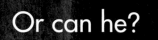

Or can he?

More *Read-it!* Readers

Bright pictures and fun stories help you practice your reading skills. Look for more books at your level.

Back to School 1-4048-1166-4
The Bath 1-4048-1576-7
The Best Snowman 1-4048-0048-4
Bill's Baggy Pants 1-4048-0050-6
Camping Trip 1-4048-1167-2
Days of the Week 1-4048-1581-3
Eric Won't Do It 1-4048-1188-5
Fable's Whistle 1-4048-1169-9
Finny Learns to Swim 1-4048-1582-1
Goldie's New Home 1-4048-1171-0
I Am in Charge of Me 1-4048-0646-6
The Lazy Scarecrow 1-4048-0062-X
Little Joe's Big Race 1-4048-0063-8
The Little Star 1-4048-0065-4
Meg Takes a Walk 1-4048-1005-6
The Naughty Puppy 1-4048-0067-0
Paula's Letter 1-4048-1183-4
Selfish Sophie 1-4048-0069-7
The Tall, Tall Slide 1-4048-1186-9
The Traveling Shoes 1-4048-1588-0
A Trip to the Zoo 1-4048-1590-2
Willy the Worm 1-4048-1593-7

Looking for a specific title or level? A complete list of *Read-it!* Readers is available on our Web site:
www.picturewindowbooks.com